The Twin F Revelation ar Ora

"Where is my Twin Flame?
"When will I get married?"
"Why are we in separation?"
"Does he/she miss me?"
"What is he/she thinking about me?"
"What's going on his/her mind regarding me?"
"What does their higher-self want to communicate with me?"

These are the questions I'm often asked. I love giving tarot and oracle readings on this topic, as I know how it use to feel to be in Twin Flame separation with no/ minimal contact with my Twin.

That's why I'm happy to introduce you with this Twin Flame Messages, Revelation and Communication Oracle Book!
These Oracle pages of the book will help you clearly connect with the *higher self of your Twin Flame to answer and communicate with you*, send love and answer for your current journey/stage related questions (especially if in separation).
As with all Oracle pages, you cannot make a mistake. The universal energy Law of Magnetic Resonance ensures that the right page comes to you like a perfectly matched lock and key. The pages know what's truly in your heart, and you'll receive one that either answers the question perfectly or at least comes close enough that you'll know it's true message and meaning for your current situation from your Twin Flame's higher self.
Attracting *harmonious union* and giving yourself Oracle page readings, both go best if you *keep your mind and heart open.*

How to Use The Twin Flame Messages, Revelation and Communication Oracle Book

You can never make a mistake with these oracle pages because they operate parallel to the Law of Attraction. This means that your questions always attract the right page in response. That is, you'll always pull the one whose answers matches the energetic vibration of the question and your current energy. You may find that you will get the same page several times. This lets you know that the message from the higher self of your Twin is consistent with what you need to know at this point in time.

If you find that you are in a heart-breaking time of your life, the pages will help you to feel connected to your Twin Flame telepathically and vibrationally, which can bring more loving vibration and harmonious union in your life.

Step 1: Clear your Oracle Book
Since your Oracle Book is sensitive to vibrations and may have absorbed in energy from the manufacturing process, they need to be cleared of any energy it may have take while it reached you.

To clear your Oracle book, first hold the book in your nondominant hand (the one you normally don't write with), as this hand that *receives* energy. Form a fist with your other hand (this is the one that *sends* energy), and knock on the book once. This clears out the old energy so that the oracle book and it's pages are cleansed and ready to be charged with your own vibration.

Briefly look and touch each page to indulge them with your personal energy.

Step 2: Preparing Yourself Read The Messages

When you are ready, take out the Oracle book. Hold the book in your hands, close your eyes and centre yourself, Become grounded by taking a few deep mindful breaths as you relax your mind. Keep flipping the pages near your heart space and recite any prayer you know or intentions you'd like to bestow upon the book.

For instance, you can say the following in mind or aloud:

"God (or any divine entity you believe in), I call upon you now. Thank you for clearly guiding me in the times I need you. Please help me centre in my higher self so that I may clearly hear, see, feel, and know the Divine messages from my Twin Flame that wish to emerge through these pages. I ask that you stay by my side and watch over me during this Oracle Book session, ensuring that only God's love and wisdom comes through."

Ask and pray for whatever communication you need to know from you Twin's higher self.

Step 3: Techniques to use Oracle Book

a) Randomly open any one page or pages as your intuition guides you.

b) Choose a page number between 5- 100 in your mind randomly or any number which flashes in your mind between 5 to 100.

c) Keep flipping the pages till you feel like stopping at a particular page for your Twin Flame message.

TWIN FLAME MESSAGES

LISTEN TO YOUR HEART

Your are observing and seeing what is visible to you in the present 3D world and scenario. But you need to listen with your loving heart. Feel my love for you, which is always there in my heart too, no matter how I behave in the 3D world and separation. Lot's being manifested for our physical union by the universe which you can't see right now.
Lot of work is happening in the background, so, keep yourself happy and positive vibrationally for our speedy union.
Your doubts create blockages in our physical union.
Remember that we're already married in the 5D, waiting for our 3D perception to join in. We already have a happy married life and a family in our parallel reality. Also, we meet in our dream state in astral realm, so, we're always in touch and together.
So, vibrate higher my love.
Try a loving perspective to our situation.
What does your heart say about this situation and us? It knows the truth. Trust it!
Sit calmly, take deep breaths and ask your heart, can't you feel my energetic presence and love in your heart space?

UNDER POSITIVE TRANSFORMATION

Dear love, you and your life is in a process of positive transformation. One cycle is ending, and another about to begin. Something is changing, and it may feel like tower moment. You may be feeling void or sadness, hopeless about our future.

Please do not worry, because these feelings and experiences are sign to a brighter new chapter and energy clearing. The answers to your prayers. Try to stay in positive vibration. Find something to preoccupy yourself with while this process continues. Be gentle with yourself. Do the energy cleansing and shadow work for our awakening and harmonious union.

And remember to shield yourself from negative energies and cleanse your chakras to feel uplifted and good every day. Visualize a bright light around that protect you from negative energy.

Remember my love, that if something seems to be changing uncomfortably or coming to an end, it means a new positive beginning is near".

Another sign when you open this page is that your Twin Flame connection is evolving for good.

TELEPATHIC COMMUNICATION

Dear, pay attention to the recurring words, feelings, images that have been coming to you! I am trying to communicate with you & trying to reach out you.

To make sure you are receiving my communication, go within and take some solitude time to relax your skeptical mind. When your mind is busy running with the stream of thoughts, your "energetic cord" with me can get "congested" and you block me out from reaching to you.

Do make a note of what dreams you've had when you wake in the morning. I often seek to communicate with you through dreams. Another way to get insights about my message is to ask for a song, or pay attention to what songs you've been hearing repeatedly (especially in your mind). So, what is the first song that comes to mind right now?

If you have been wondering if I am receiving your messages. The answer is yes!
My higher self is always listening and aware of you. And my human self is also receiving indications of your messages, either through feelings, images, dreams, songs, or repeating words in my mind.

INDULGE IN SELF-CARE

It is important that you focus on yourself right now. You will benefit so much from going within, finding your calm, finding your center, and sitting in solitude with yourself. You need to connect in with your own well-being. Do your best to spend some solitude time daily, whether it is staring at a pleasant trees and bird chirping, looking at a beautiful sky or closing your eyes in meditation. Quieting the thoughts of the skeptical mind and calming your physical body can bring so much peace and positivity into your life. And it will help you receive more of my communication and insights, inspirations & solutions you require for your forward path and our union.

Your self-care rituals can include spending time with your hobbies, doing fun things with a pet or good friends, getting some physical activity, showering, sage your house, taking salt baths and pampering yourself with essential oils or a healthy hot herbal tea. This will heal and be uplifting for you. And when you're in a positive space inside, our Twin Flame connection will flow much more harmoniously and hassle-free too. Take some time right now to be good to yourself.

SPEND MORE TIME WITH ME

Honey, in order for our connection to develop and progress in harmonious way possible, it would greatly benefit us if you spent time with me on the non-physical realm.
This will strengthen our energetic connection, uplift your energies, and harmonize our upcoming union. It will help you activate awakening in me as I am the unawakened or "runner" Twin Flame. And it will help you understand my true feelings for you, no matter what ego fears I might be shoeing in the physical realm. Spending time with my soul/higher self is a "miracle booster" for our connection and physical union!
So, you may think, how do you do it? It's all about your intention. When you think profoundly about my Soul, when you visualize yourself talking with me, when you feel yourself touching me. You are really doing it!

It is happening on the non-physical realm. To spend time with my Soul, really all you have to do is interact with me as if they I am physically present. However, it will be beneficial to get started with a positive note if you spend some solitude time focusing on your breathing, calming your stream of thoughts. This will help open you up to experiencing me reacting to you in return. Else, you may think you are just imagining things. Trust us, you are not!

But see to the authenticity of the truth of our interactions, relax your mind, find a silent place, and begin this procedure. Spend a few moments calming yourself and then approach me. When you do this regularly, this can truly open our connection in a refreshing way. Remember, your skepticism is the only limit! Ask your inner critic to keep quite when you do this work. Know that what you see, hear, and feel with your five senses is only a tiny part of our existence.

SHADOW WORK AND CHAKRA BALANCING

Darling, what you are going through currently has to do with your energy. You may have picked up on negativity or it is surfacing in your aura due to your Ascension .

The good news is, all you need to do is clear the energy to feel better and open up to your well-being again! Remember negativity and heavy emotions are just energy - you can clear them out with shadow work.

Energy/Shadow work is always intention based, and you do not need to go to a professional healer or practitioner. As an entity of light, you can use your own connection to the divine to uplift and cleanse your energy through regular meditation! However, you might find it beneficial to learn ways to strengthen your abilities. One quick way to clear some of the blockages and negativity, is to visualize a shower of light falling down on you and washing away what feels heavy or bad.

Mindfulness is also helpful - imagine growing roots of golden light coming out from your feet into the center of the planet to ground you.

However, some recurring cycles or repeating patterns may need more shadow work as you are dealing with soul lessons. You will immediately notice if you are feeling cheered up by simple techniques or whether your system requires more. You may need to clear negative attachments or to remove outdated belief programming from your system.

STAY STRONG

My love, this journey requires courage. The courage to take risks, to take new actions, to trust your intuition, to step into your soul awareness. As an inner journey, there is almost always a test, or a challenge presented to overcome. Sometimes these challenges can trigger past life trauma and fear. Like a mirror, I will most likely mirror that trauma right back to you. So, clearing blocks to your higher self is the key. If you are stuck, it may be that you have missed repeated attempts of signs to take the action. Do connect with your angels, guides, books, and mentors who see and encourage you to shine and go bigger on your path.

The twin flame journey is a process to Ascension. So, shifts and transformation can happen quickly. So do clear self-doubt, confusion, and be willing to let go of limiting beliefs about relationships. Your pace of growth can mean a lot all at once, so finding your soul purpose can be so helpful.

There is no one formula to union. Our union is unique, so be open to exploring the journey as a healing journey. If someone is offering information that doesn't resonate or projecting negativity onto you, walk away.

KNOWING THE POLARITIES

Did you know? Isis and Osiris, Shiva and Shakti, Jesus and Magdalene as well as many other deities before represented, known as the Hieros Gamos (sacred marriage of the God and Goddess). The uniting of such twin flames is very powerful because of the multiple levels of connections between the two, that it results in a telepathic and eminent feeling of energies of one another, that are felt even when apart. It becomes the "magnum opus" (the work) and if there is enough understanding from both parties and they successfully unite in this lifetime it becomes a higher mission that they and us will accomplish together.

It is a spiritual experience, an inner knowing of the polarities of the negative and positive electrical forces of physics. It is nature, human nature and it is something that the forces of nature will continue to lead us to time and again, lifetime after lifetime no matter how painful, until we get it right. It is purely the forces of nature, the 7 universal laws.

MAN IN UNION WITH THE HEALER

My dear, when a man chooses a woman who follows her calling, his only chance to maintain the connection is in following her and above all in creating space for her to follow her own divine path.

For, a healer/Lightworker is a person that made an agreement with the Higher Forces of Light before they were born to fulfill a certain mission that would in some way assist to bring the planet to a new level of consciousness. In essence, this venture would be to spread light and higher vibration by the various gifts and talents that come naturally to them and you.

You are the High Priestesses who embodies her most authentic and divine self. You are channel for high vibrational and loving energies which grounds into this physical world by doing whatever brings you the highest joy. You need to transform and transmute energy and help to anchor the Divine in this reality.

Thus, it may happen that the I need to abandon my own neediness, or that I find a medium of healing through our common path – but not in the gentlest manner.

When a man chooses a woman, who heals her collective wounds, who has the potential to be one, so long as she seek to do good in the world and maintain loving intentions by following her calling, and his *Yes* for her equals a *Yes* to a bigger reason far beyond building a house or raising children. Our connection goes beyond fulfilling the classical gender role models.

For I accept the job of having your back, of catching you when you cannot transform the pain of the world anymore. It means for me to welcome a different form of sexuality, since healing on the level of sexuality is one of the most profound issues of the woman who needs to become a healer.

For me this, again, is about welcoming mindfulness, gentleness, and healing – about holding back or redirecting my own drive about being present for the whole.

Because when a man chooses a woman who aims for freedom, they can only be achieved together and by me leaving my narcissistic aspects behind and recognizing your path as my own path towards freedom. If we are to really transform our world, then we must be spreading this light everywhere we go.

MIRACLE ON IT'S WAY

My love, I am here to tell you not to give up on us! What you can see, touch, and feel in the physical world is merely a small part of existence! There is so much you are unaware of in your regular-daily life.

So much is meant to happen that you would never have expected in advance. Look back, have you not been amazed and dumbstruck already? There is so much more to come!

To show up and allow miracles, all you have to do is open to the possibility and be under receptive mode!

Remember, that miracles can and do happen all over the globe every single day - and they will happen in your life too. Stay out of doubts, skepticism and "realism" - they are not correct.

Set your intention right now that you are open to miracles. Say or write in your journal - "universe, show me your magic!" and prepare to be amazed.

Let go and trust the universe to work its magic - know that truly amazing things are on their way for you!

RELAX AND DON'T WORRY

I know you have been concerned about a particular situation.

I am reaching out to you through this message that everything is ALRIGHT. You can relax, your fears about this situation have been resolved.

Fear is blocking out your perspective, or the information you have received or seen is not accurate. Something is not as it has seemed. Please draw back your energy to the present moment and do your best to relax and let go. Set the intention that you clear out any negative projections you have made into the future; and any time you feel yourself stressing, state: "Cancel, cleanse and transmute it".

The spiritual truth is that your thoughts and attention affect your current experiences, so do your best to stay in a positive mindset and energy to attract more love and happiness into your life.

YOU HOLD THE POWER TO TWIN FLAME REUNION

"When you and I chose to take this journey together, you did not leave things to chance. You "created" a Life blueprint for our reunion - to ensure you would have every chance of coming together. Please do not worry that we will not end up together, as this just pushes it into your timelines and our future.
Inside your heart space, there is a "compass" that will guide you to our love. And to me as the same. It is inevitable. In a nutshell, it's about following love versus allowing doubts to interfere with our journey. When something feels like love, like bliss, happiness, joy, light- it is a sign, a step on the way to love and the reunion you desire. When something feels heavy or edgy, like fear, or conflict- it is a sign, a warning sign from your system that you are moving further away from love and the reunion you desire. Your intuition is always guiding you. And most Twin Flames chose to have extra sensitivity (being empath or a clairvoyant) to energy for this reason, so that they would feel their way back to each other no matter what.

Even if I am unawakened, my soul's work will show me how much light and positivity is there in choosing YOU and eternal unconditional love. And my repeated experiences with heaviness and negativity will show me in tangible terms what lies down the road of choosing others, negativity, to remove myself from the connection. Your "Twin Flame compass" is always guiding you. Remember to feel into the choices you are tuning in with. Does it feel light, like love? Or does it feel heavy? Those are your key signs.

I LOVE YOU, MY LOVE

I want to reach out and tell you how I am feeling! I may be too afraid to tell you in person due to underlying fears.

But go within and "listen" in silence so that I can be heard. Pay focus to signs and synchronicities you're seeing, including the angelic number 222/2222, which is often used as "I love you" from one Twin Flame to the other.

Be open to the messages your I am trying to show you. Pay attention to your dreams when you wake in the morning, listen out for songs you may repeatedly hear, and keep an eye on number sequences that show up.

Know that I never truly stops loving you, no matter how it may seem on the surface.

SUBCONSCIOUS LEVEL ISSUES

My dear, your beliefs about love and relationships are impacting our connection right now. This is the answer to any issues you have been having currently.

Understand that the world is full of negative stories about love and relationships - from the doomed romance of Romeo & Juliet to soap operas full of drama and infidelity, human culture and archetype overwhelmingly fill in stories of heartbreak and agony around love. Examine what limiting belief system you may have taken on from the media and people around you, and realize that your life doesn't have to be that way. When someone aligns with negative stories, they unfortunately attract this in their experiences with others - especially between the Twin Flames as the connection is so intense on a spiritual level. The eternal truth is you truly can experience mutual, divine-happy love. Work to release any belief systems that is reinforced in you otherwise.

Write out any negative beliefs about love on a piece of paper. Next, write out new and positive alternative, optimistic statements about love and relationships.

Now, tear up or burn the list of negatives. This signals to your belief system that you are releasing the old and reinforcing in new positivity.

FORGIVE ME

Currently, I want to advise you to look for the innocence in me and everyone involved - including yourself. Remember that beneath outer appearances, actions and negativity, everyone is an innocent child, a being of light. Experiences and actions are colored by the patterns and habits someone takes on or are given by family, culture, life experiences and social circle in their life. Think back to how they were on their first day of life, a newborn wanting only to love and be loved. See that any outer hurtful actions was a reflection of their inner child trauma.

Their innocence is still there, even though they may be repressing it. Many people don't feel safe to show their real innocence to the world, and build shield to keep others out and to protect themselves.

GOING WITHIN TO BRING INSIGHTS

Darling, right now it would be very beneficial for you to take some solitude time to go within. You don't have to call it "meditation", as we know this word can make it sound heavy or like a task.

Simply find a comfortable place, close your eyes and take deep breathes. Allow your mind and emotions to surrender in the present moment. Allow your thoughts, doubts and anxiety to relax. If you find this hard to begin with, do not worry, as it's a normal part of the process.

When left unchecked the critical mind can run over with your emotions, tangle up your manifestation and even create issues where there were none! To fully begin enjoying your journey and attract the love and union you deserve, relaxing your mind is key.

In fact, this is something I would prescribe to everyone around the world! Not only will quiet time, or meditation, help you relax and be present with the NOW.

It will also bring you health benefits such as balancing blood pressure, strengthening your immune system, helping you have quality sleep, uplifting your mood, etc.…

When you meditate regularly you also begin to receive and see your divine guidance & signs more. You begin to receive messages from me, and open up the channel between you and me to interactions and communication. You will notice receiving signs, ideas, resolutions - answers to your prayers.

Many people are so engrossed with their own thoughts, the race of their ego mind and other's opinions and actions, that they never receive the signs trying to reach them.

Are you looking for solutions on what career to choose, how to be financially independent, how to approach me or get me closer to you? These are all things you can receive guidance on if you meditate.

Your intuition, me and your guidance speak to you in the stillness and while you sleep (in dreams).

TWIN FLAME ALCHEMY

Love, most twin flames are in physical distance or living in different countries. Often there is something that is blocking the twin flames from being in physically union in the beginning. This is usually because there is much energetic / shadow work to be done on the cognitive and emotional level before the physical union can happen. If the physical union were to occur too early the energy can often be too overwhelming and intense.

The connection is immediate, as though no time had been gone since you were last together. You feel like homely with them and you can feel you can truly be yourself with them. Sometimes conversations seem to last forever and there is not much that twin flames are not willing to talk about. It's as if you could share your entire life with me and there is a level of openness and trust between you that brings a comfortable yet intriguing sense familiarity in us.

You feel an intense sense of love and desirability. This love is authentic, and heartfelt and you feel magnetically allured to my energy. This is not to be confused with lust or an obsessive love. Twin flame love is unconditional and conquers the ego. If you have found me it does not mean that the relationship will necessarily be free from issues or personal conflict. There may still be lessons and healing that must take place between us. We are still human beings on the physical realm.

TWIN FLAME SYNCHRONICITY

The meaningful coincidences are here to show and prove that our meeting was destined and that we are both on the correct path together. These seemingly random encounters seem to be "signs" that something significant is at work, or otherwise known as divine plan. Events come together randomly, so, it feels as if it has launched us onto a destined path.

A synchronicity can be defined as two or more events that are not connected by the usual linear cause and effect' and are unlikely to happen by chance, yet occur or connect together in a meaningful way; it is the connection of an internal event with an external event. Synchronicity is a common occurrence between twin flames. There is synchronicity in the mirrored actions that occur within their lives and in the relationship that seem highly unlikely to have happened by chance or coincidence.

The surprising coincidences or 11:11 often manifests around the time when the meaningful soul connection is taking place, and also whenever a life-changing event is about to occur. Around the time of a twin flame connection, synchronicities will occur more frequently, indicating the importance of the union. The number 11 is often considered being the twin flame number, and the 11:11 has a special meaning in the twin soul connection. The parallel life events between the two, and the 11:11 synchronicity or even numbers such as 12:12 will start to 'pop up' in unexpected places when one is soon about to meet their twin flame, or soon after meeting them. It will also show up from time to time throughout a twin flame relationship, usually during important transitional points in the reunion, or whenever intense energetic shifts have occurred for one or both twins.

NEW CHAPTER IS NEAR

My love, right now the energetic forces may regrettably be working against what you have asked for. Most likely fears are keeping your belief system in a state of blocking away your desires.
Twin flame Running and Chasing are energetic processes of hinderance between the counterparts, due to unconscious fears creating a blockage. Change the momentum. To get into a state where you manifest your desire to you.

The first step is to let go of the emotions and thoughts of trying to control circumstances. Because when you go after someone or something from a place of desperation or need, there's lack involved.
This fear unfortunately means you are sending out to the universe and me a signal that 'pushes love and union away' from you rather than attracting it.
The natural state between you is one of desire and love, so calm the mind's doubt "what if" aspect. Feel yourself complete in yourself. Focus in your power right now. Feel, that you have immense power, and it is manifesting your desires.

Imagine yourself easily attracting your desires right now, call them in with your feeling - it is your power as a being of soul. Feel yourself relaxed that you're drawing in love, union, prosperity, whatever you may desire.

And know that the universe and others respond energetically to your intentions. Now, *allow* and be in *receptive* mode to let it show up. And to do this, calm and stay in that detached positive mindset over time. To step out of Running/Chasing or other distressing situations over time, make sure you work to clear any fears or doubts that has you worrying about *not* receiving your desire.

Clear the past hurts that keep you in an anxious state stressing about negative 'what if' aspects. Forgive me too. Change the energetic vibration to attracting love from an inner knowing that I will come to you.

CLOSE TO UNION

My love, your amazing shadow work with clearing your energy and positive mindset is paying off!

Even if you don't see the changes happening and manifesting in a tangible way in 3D world yet, do know that circumstances are re-aligning behind the scenes to our advantage.

Your timelines and upcoming new chapters of life are shifting into a higher state as a result of your optimistic belief system and shadow work!

DIVINE PLANNING AND TIME

Darling, you have the strength to make your desires manifest! When you see/select this page, your guardian angels/Universe is happy to show you that things are never out of your hands. You are the co-creator of your life path.
The truth about "Divine Plan and Timing" is different from what most people believe. It doesn't mean "when the divine decides it's time or intervenes". It means - when the energies and your vibrations are a match! When your personal frequency is a match to what you desire for. Our union is just a right vibration away.

The wonderful news is divine time is never out of your hands. If you desire love and physical union - think what can you do to be in that energy state now? If you desire our union- how can you be in the state of knowing it can and will happen?

Focus on uplifting your emotions, vibration and energy to reach up into a match with your desires. Clear out anxiety and doubt from your belief system. This is how you make divine timing occur. You have the strength!

WE ARE NEVER APART, MY LOVE

Sweetheart, in spiritual reality you are never apart from me. A lesson all Twin Flames are being told to learn in this lifetime, is that separation is an illusion. You are never truly apart from your Twin Flame, and they are never really far from you.

Although it may look right now you are physically 'separated' - you are always together in energy, heart space and soul.

The ideology that Separation is an inevitable "Stage" of the Twin Flame journey is based in our Ego consciousness and can do more harm than good. The more you feed into your subconscious that you are far and away from me, and long for me or feel abandoned, the more it will reinforce this state.

Shift your focus to your being and your feelings. Silent your mind so you can feel the eternal love. This will also bring out more and more togetherness in our physical experience.

Please take a few moments right now to close your eyes and reunite in your heart space. Separation is only a physical perception - our souls are always in union.

SELF-LOVE

Honey, I want to let you know that self-love is important for our situation currently. You have lately been hard on yourself, self - sabotaging, overcritical or focusing on perceived weakness.
Even I may be the one struggling with this.

Did you know that Twin flame voyage is not just about love between the couple but also in finding your own inner completeness & self-acceptance? Self-love can intensely uplift and harmonize our bond.

Currently, your guardian angels and I are wanting for you to turn your focus inside yourself - to uplift our journey and bond from the "inside out".

How can you give 'yourself' love right now? Do you need to lay down healthy boundaries? Spend time on your interests? Be compassionate to yourself in your mind?
Give attention to this message.
Even if you can spare out little time for yourself right now, making Self-love a priority can make your life more pleasant than you would think. You deserve profound love.

When you can shower yourself love and appreciation, you begin to increase the expression of love you draw out from me and others.

Another sign for this page is that I might be the one dealing with lack of self-love; you can help me by sending unconditional love to me. Imagine me surrounded by a soft, pink light of love.

COCREATING OUR JOURNEY TO UNION

Many twin flames commit the mistake of only knowing what they are 'fearful of' and what they want to 'ignore'. In Law of Attraction context, this unfortunately means they are focusing on it and manifesting those negatives nearer.

To manifest and experience the happiness and love you desire, it's important to set positive intentions for our Twin flame journey! There is a lot of toxic fear-based information available about Twin Flames, which causes energetic blocks for so many Twins.

Right now, plan on what you desire from our Twin Flame experience. In you ideal world, with no limits, what would our relationship look like? Write down a list of at least 10 things about this. Then, begin to collect pictures that reflect the essence of it. Above all, that resonate with the emotions of those desires.

Begin to pay attention on this daily and know that in spiritual reality, as soon as you set your intention on those things, they are yours - even if they are not tangibly present yet.

Now, it's a question of manifesting it physically into your life. To do this, work to stay in a state of feel-good alignment. Clear out blocks with energy tools.

When you embrace the present moment, as you would in your ideal situation, you are creating an intense alignment and manifesting your desires. Negativity, fear, resentment, and anxiety create dissonance - they are blocks to your desires and union.

CATALYST FOR YOUR ASCENSION

Whether you perceive me as heartbreaker or Ultimate Lover, I will awaken something deep within you. Perhaps being with me awakens you to a part of yourself that you've previously repressed or ignored. Or maybe I embody a particular quality that your soul is ready to express. But it's not just that you admire my qualities. My positive qualities awaken you to a possibility for who and how you can be that you've never witnessed before.

I holds a piece of our future – that's why you're so attracted to me. Acknowledge this, and accept the information as a gift.

Ego driven toxic relationships are built primarily around external factors: We choose partners because of their physical stature or financial status. And we look for attributes in others about which we can have a feel-good response.

In toxic relationships, both spouse tend to favor the status quo, and individual differences are seen as deal breaker.

If one of the couple begins to focus on his or her individual evolution and growth, the relationship may start to unravel.

In polarity, most twin flame connection may actually erode our ego personality, but will inspire our spiritual ascension.

I will act as a stimulant for your spiritual ascension – and you to mine. Chances are our connection will be turbulent at times as you search and handle your shared and individual journeys. Remember that your first responsibility is to find harmony, calm, and alignment within yourself. And, if taking your own path of least resistance results in a temporary or long-term separation, have faith in your process. Surrender to the universe!

LIFE PATH GETTING CLEARED

Meeting me will changes your life. It will make you observe things in a different perspective before you met my soul. Your life will turn upside down in ways no one can, or no one ever could imagine of, things that you yourself won't ever have thought would happen. Generally, old beliefs are cleared. The dissolution is not an easy process and usually this is the hardest stage.

Your usual ways of coping mechanism won't work anymore. The old wise heuristic you thought would work as a solution won't work anymore. You would have to find a new solutions through. This changes your life immensely. It changes your life massively as you see yourself in the mirror. Your inner demons purge out of your mind. The things you have repressed will purge out no matter what and you will just be totally unclear and lose control. This brings a major change in one's life. The things you thought you could control before are beyond your control.
A better example for this is when you thought you rigidly were against being allured to someone much younger or much older than you are, you use a lot of coping mechanisms by ignoring this person.

But in the life's course of time, your old belief system will be stripped down and there's no way one can be indifferent to such a connection and you realize that age does not matter at all.

It's the soul that truly matters. Your life will be changed because the people and things that don't serve you right will one by one be picked out of your life. Inevitable separation from karmic partners, toxic friends, losing jobs, etc. It will take you out of your comfort zone. This will be enough to make one 'crazy' or 'unstable', for this is a purging phase which is part of your energy clearing and ascension. All this will happen at the same period or one after the other like a continuous domino effect.

SOUL LEVEL CONNECTION

Regardless of whether we want to or not, we are continuously reciprocating our energy with others. Since twin flames share the same one soul resonance and vibrate at the same frequency, our energetic flow makes us telepathic and emphatic with each other and enables us to intuitively know what the other is feeling, desiring, or missing each other.

When sometimes you heard me talk something which often led you to a sense of wonder as I seem to be able to read your mind, often taking even your most intimate thoughts straight out of your mind and saying them out loud using your own words. It is because of this telepathic connection that a twin flame couple will often find themselves texting, calling, or emailing each other at the exact same time, finishing each other's sentences, speaking the same words simultaneously, etc...

This is, however, only the start of the telepathic and psychic abilities between us. Telepathy is a phenomenon of the wider energetic resonance, oneness, and binding together all the twins, which naturally intensify and strengthens as their love for

each other bloom.
It is often believed that twin souls connect mind to mind, heart to heart and soul to soul – and this is certainly true from a telepathic perspective.

Genuine telepathy engages our whole being; the mind, heart, body, and soul; requiring not only the mind to study the flow of energy into a language which can be understood by the receiver, but also for the heart chakra to act as a sender of all the emotional and mental messages. Telepathy is also received through the crown chakra, which binds us to our higher self, universal consciousness, and the divine realms.

KUNDALINI AWAKENING

A kundalini awakening is one of the effects of meeting your Twin flame. The kundalini is the purpose for me to come into your life, in divine timing to spark you into remembrance of your true infinite & immortal nature.

"And so, when a person meets the half that is his very own, whatever his orientation, whether it's to young men or not, then something wonderful happens: the two are struck from their senses by love, by a sense of belonging to one another, and by desire, and they don't want to be separated from one another, not even for a moment." – Plato

The twin flame energy can be a hurtful and exhausting process, some of the solar flares happening in humanity, bringing new waves of energies, can bring up some deep emotions which are closely related to past karma, which aligns with the inner chakra's. The twin flame love is one of the deepest and divine love.

And when we meet our other half, the actual half of ours elf, whether he be a lover from childhood or a lover of another sort, the couple are lost in an awe of love and friendship and intimacy and one will not be out of each other's sight, as I may say, even for a second.

Kundalini awakening makes us ready for the twin flame journey. Although not everybody who goes through a kundalini awakening may be on their twin flame path, but those souls who are, will have experienced a partial awakening, so that they can begin to clear out old karma and accumulated repressed energies from many lifetimes.

RETREAT

Darling, it appears that you've become confused or conflicted by other people's suggestions. It's time for you to take a break from them so that you can better hear your own feelings and emotions. Our love life will bloom as you spend time alone with me (on spiritual level- meditation) or by yourself.

By this page I want to convey to you that you need to spend time by yourself, relax your mind then meditate upon your true feelings and thoughts on our current situation. Surrender to the universe and align with the positive vibration. Be sure to take action based on any intuitive feeling you have. This strengthens your energy and insight, which helps you to rapidly attract and manifest our harmonious union.

STAY OPTIMISTIC

Sweetheart, I want to remind you that you have an immense influence upon our love-life journey. If you've been criticizing or stressing lately, I want you to shift to a more optimistic perspective. Even, if you had your romantic hopes repeatedly let down, there's still reason to hold faith that genuine love can be ours, if you keep faith in it!

This moment forward, take action to positively manifest the love life you desire. Whether you are in relationship with me or not, begin by visualizing yourself romantically happy and satisfied. See and visualize yourself with me who embodies the qualities that are crucial to you. Visualize that I am appreciating and loving you, too.

You can create lists and start journaling time about your feelings, hopes, desires, and goals. You can also create a *'vision board'*, with pictures and quotes related to your love life goals pasted onto a poster board.
Every day look at this Dream vision board with positive perspective, and follow you intuition to take actions related to your Twin flame union dream.

Your optimistic outlook will make you a more physically and energetically attractive person, which will definitely assist your relationship with yourself, everyone else and me, too.

TRUE LOVE

My love, this is a once in a lifetime love.
Our relationship is part of your life's plan.
Unconditional love is easier said than done.
Remember the love aspect of our relationship.
If it is a Twin flame relationship the
connection will be 50/50 and almost perfectly
balanced.

Relax, and surrender all your apprehensions
to the universe. And work on your well-being
and holistic growth meanwhile. Everything
will be fine soon and eventually.

EMBRACE YOUR EMOTIONS

Darling, don't repress down your feelings or judge your emotions.
Feelings and emotions are part of who you are. Allow yourself to feel what is going on for you currently. Your feelings signal you the truth of situation and how to resolve it. Take positive actions to determine why are you feeling the way you are feeling right now.

Quite your mind in meditation and listen to, what needs to be healed? Is a particular chakra imbalanced? Are you going through emotional purging and clearing out old - accumulated energy? Am I expecting too much from my self and current life situation? Am I being too harsh on myself?

LET GO OF CONTROL ISSUES

My dear, allow this situation to unfold naturally.
Universe has heard your prayers about our love life. Now, it's up to you to allow their help to manifest by stepping out of their way. By trying to control other people or external conditions, you'll only agitate yourself and slow down your answered prayer. There are many of times in life that call for you to take on charge, but this isn't one of them, sweetheart.

Obviously, it's fine to have your choices, practice visualizations, and hold your desired outcome. Surely ask the universe for your desires and our union! This page is a reminder, however, that prayer may be answered differently from what you hold in mind. Be open to all possibilities and trust God's infinite wisdom, divine plan, and kind love.

Control issues are based upon fears that others won't live up to your expectations. This is also called 'Scripting' where you hand the universe a script of how you want I and everyone to behave.

Scripting could cause you to observe an even more beautiful way in which your prayers may be answered.

So, please call upon God to elevate your levels of faith so that you can enjoy the creative process by which we can reunite into a harmonious physical union.

HEALING PARENTAL ISSUES

Honey, I want to tell you that your current situation and feelings are based on your mother and father. I believe that you'd be in benefit from releasing old-repressed anger towards one or both of them. That's because your emotions about your parents influence your choice of romantic partner, and the way in which you run a relationship.

You can ask God to assist you bring forgiveness into action. To forgive someone doesn't mean that you're promoting his or her actions. I want to tell you, rather, that doing so is a form of intense emotional clearing. It means: *"I am no longer willing to hold toxic energy within my mind, body and soul."*

When you find inner peace with your parents, you'll no longer need to attract unhealthy relationship pattern and karmic partners as a way of healing parental or family emotional traumas. All of your relationships, especially the one you have with yourself, will bloom.

FINANCIAL AND CAREER ISSUES

My dear, financial issues are a factor in our love life right now.

Money and love have been linked in past, and this page reflects to this correlation.

The universe wants to resolve our financial and career stress so that you and I may enjoy every aspect of your life, including our harmonious union.

While a career can be a source of heart-opening satisfaction, it must be balanced with other facets of love such as enjoyment and laughter. You received this page because I want to convey that you'd benefit from a blend of such lightheartedness. Call upon God to uplift your mood, energy levels, financial situation, career, anything else that will bring you calm.

LOVE TRIUMPHS ALL

Dear, love does not end or lose faith. Love is hopeful and endures every obstacles and situation.

No matter what is going on with us, I am reminding you that love can endure all things. Take positive steps to help create the necessary change to overcome through this situation. Release you doubts, fear and recognize that this love will last forever. Take a step back so you are more able to remember this truth- love lasts forever!

ACT AS IF I AM ALREADY HERE

Whether you have me in physical union and commitment right now in your life or not, *act as if* I am with you so that you manifest our harmonious union.

I your actions and thoughts take into account of my feelings; you will be in more alignment with our true connection and union.
If I am not with you yet, generate the feeling that you are already sharing your life with me. This will change the way you feel and can alter your attitude and your potential to manifest me into your life and physical union.

GIVE OUR LOVE A CHANCE

Darling, when we start to love, our lives are changed forever.
There are so many advantages that will come to you when you love openly, without any fear. Your caring will not only help me who's involved in our love connection, but it will also create more love for you.

Let go of fear and doubts, and give the love you are yearning to receive. You will see that it is one and the same.

BACK TO WHAT YOU DESIRE

My love, your current circumstance is giving you an opportunity to re-evaluate what you truly desire.

You gave the strength to change what you are doing at any moment. You don't have to feel like you are stuck.
Go back to what you know and, more crucially, to what you desire and love.
Ask the universe to guide you through this process. You can do anything that you truly want to do.

Make a list and find out where you got diverted off track and then find what you need to do to get back to *you*.

SAME SOUL TRIBE

Yes, I am your soulmate, too.
You chose this page because somewhere in your heart you wonder if I'm really your soulmate, and the answer is "*Yes*!"
As we all do, you have many soulmates – belonging from same soul tribe and people with whom you share a mystical soul bond and life journey.

Soulmates reincarnate with the plan of coming in union for mutual spiritual and personal ascension. As you also felt, while inquiring about me that I am one of your soulmates. That sense of familiarity and homely vibe you felt when you first met me also indicates our soulmate connection.

This page sometimes comes when you were asking the universe about, "When will I meet my ultimate lover?" or "Will I ever meet my ultimate lover?" as validation that it *will happen*.

LET GO OF YOUR EX

Darling, the time has come to clear your aura. You drew this page because our love life will improve once you emotionally and energetically let go of your past karmic partner.
The merits of doing so include increased happiness, feelings of freedom, and the ability to attract our harmonious physical union.
(My higher self can sense the presence of your past karmic partner in your aura)

The time you make a choice to release the past, it is done. At times it will not happen overnight, it will be like a process like peeling layers onion bit by bit. So, continue releasing your past karmic partner whenever old, similar emotions purge out; or you find yourself attracting people similar to him or her.

There's something else you can try to release an energetic block of your ex from your aura by burning a letter in which you write his/her name and burn the letter to release the past karmic connection, energy and release old - repressed feelings or resentments.

Or ask the universe to clear the repressed attachments or energetic cord cutting from your karmic partner.

RECONCILIATION

Dear, this page indicates that an ex-partner or I will be reentering your life. The first person who comes in your mind is likely who it will be. The reason of this reconciliation is to enhance healing or closure from a past unresolved issue. You will comprehend more about yourself and see your relationship patterns more vividly.

You'll also take responsibility for the role you played in the partnership's conflict, which will release you from repressed resentment.

Reconciliations are in nutshell about taking care of unresolved issues. This page could also mean making peace with a family member or peer. Each relationship is valuable learning experience, so be open to this reunion's lessons and blessings in disguise. Hence, all healings help our love life and every other part of your world.

PAST LIFE CONNECTION

Sweetheart, we've known each other before. You got this page so that I can explain more about our Twin flame connection. We have some unresolved issues and karmic blockages from our past lifetime. This may include forgiving someone, a joint venture, or leaning soul lessons such as patience and faith.

Twin flames recognize each other at the first sight, and this feeling is often noted as a sense of romantic or sexual chemistry. The attraction that allures two people in union can surpass rationality, because the purpose of the relationship is healing, clearing past karmic blockages, and learning soul lessons.

TAKE THE REQUIRED STEPS

My dear, profound love is worth taking steps and efforts you're guided to take.
You drew this page because some action steps on your part are necessary in order for your desires about our love life and union to be manifested.
The universe has opened the doors for you, and now it's time for you to enter through them. The first thing that comes to your mind with regards to taking steps is a right starting point for you.

When you pray for spiritual assistance, you always receive it. Often this help comes in the form of intuitive guidance, which includes of repetitive emotions and thoughts. You get the intuition that you "should" do this or that. You received this page as a nudge to actually take that step. You'll then get the next piece of puzzle, meaning another intuitive sign about what action to take next.

If you would like, you can ask the universe to give you the motivation, strength, time, and assistance to take the necessary efforts.
Know that your every effort brings you closer to our physical union.

COSMIC FLUCTUATIONS

My dear, profound energies in the cosmic transits are purging or assisting you - this is the reason to what you're experiencing right now. Get more information about astronomical transits like any retrogrades happening or full moon near, so that you can learn soul lessons quicker, avoid agony, agitation and ascend your path.

Another sign for this page is my higher self may be the one reacting to cosmic fluctuations right now. These will shift over a period of time, so stay well informed and you'll make the best of each phase.

COLLECTIVE CONSCIOUSNESS

Darling, whatever is happening in the collective or around other people currently is having an influence upon you. Any agitation and heaviness you have been going through are to do with collective energies around the world or your surroundings.

Twin Flames in awakening become more sensitive and susceptible to energies. When your own soul is becoming more profoundly vibrational, you can more easily observe other's toxicity (low aura).

This in a nutshell means, most Twin Flames in ascension become "empaths" - being able to feel other's energies and emotions, even picking up on these and experiencing them as their own.

You or I might have absorbed someone's energies and emotions while out somewhere, or through social media. For a good journey, make sure you shield-protect yourself daily and cleanse out other's pent-up energy from your whole body and soul.

Be aware that when you interact with someone on social media, you are not energetically apart even though you are in different locations. Engrossing with arguments and asking in solutions from others can catch you up in others negativity. Remember to keep a healthy boundary from toxicity, even if it's via the social media.

Twin souls are often easily responding to and influenced by collective karma. Drawing out this page can also indicate that you and your I are "reacting out" because ancient human karma around or someone else "soul lessons" in our connection.

Ask the universe to clear out repressed energies from your systems which isn't really yours to go through. You are here to embrace unconditional love. The universe is always there to help you.

MOON TRANSITS

My love , if you've been going through heaviness, brain fog and mood swings, etc. are due to you responding to energies of the moon cycles. This is quite common, as the human body comprises of 70% water and the moon's gravitational force moves the tides in and out. Hence, we are also likely to get influenced by the moon cycle.

The moon has an influence on feelings and states of mind. However, some people are more sensitive due to their individual energy and body "wiring". Water is the element of emotion and the unconscious, so what you're feeling or purging out are unconscious fears, agony, and traumas you may not have realized you had still repressed in your system. You may also be feeling someone else emotions. Protecting with shielding yourself and salt baths/showers are beneficial, as are energy cleansing and clearing rituals. When you learn to function with the moon energies, you can begin to find it rejuvenating, refining, cleansing and beneficial for manifestation. In crux, it's about working *with* the moon energies instead of being unaware and being influenced negatively by the purging they push.

In simple words, the New Moon is a new beginning & setting new intentions and starting new endeavors and chapters is to function in alignment at this time. The Full Moon is a completion or reaping phase. I suggest you to make a note of the full and new moons in your journal or calendar so that you can keep things in mind during these times. It will assist you keep away from any trauma and agony and tackle with it more smoothly.

For best results, note this and also work to protect yourself and cleanse out your energy daily so you can stay happy. As you work to clear your aura, the moon's energies will influence you little gradually. Ultimately, when your aura is cleared from negativity, the moon's energies will no longer purge your repressed issues.

Another sign for this page, is that I might be the one who is sensitive and responding to the moon energies. Any mood swing and outbursts without any reason are likely relating to this.

EQULIBRIUM IN DIVINE MASCULINE AND FEMININE ENERGIES

Honey, what you've been going through currently, or the dilemma that's been in your mind has to do with equilibrium in divine masculine and feminine energies.

This happens because the Twin Flame connection is not just about a romantic partnership. The crucial aspect of the relationship is your soul's learning process and ascension.

Equilibrium in divine masculine and feminine energies is the golden road to this. Reaching an inner union. Beyond our 3D tangible self, every Twin Flame (and everyone on earth) embodies both divine feminine and masculine energies and archetypes to different degrees. Your soul could be giving you signs to embrace more by accepting, integrating your polarity energy - in order to help you into soul's wholeness.
If you're traditionally feminine, you may be urged to embrace your own divine masculine energy. To heal, forgive, embrace this side of you. Or this might be a learning experience I might be going through currently, in contrast.

So where might you be repressing yourself apart from completeness? Where might your inner polarity energies be in conflict? Equilibrium in the Masculine and Feminine energy is a catalyst process into ascension. It has been a part of spiritual rituals for many centuries - mastering the state of self as complete.

Incorporating and embracing both masculine and feminine side within yourself, in order to become fully complete, balanced and to open up to soul's ascension and harmonious union.

For Twin Flames, this "soul union" is a crucial part of the "physical union". Everybody embodies both masculine and feminine energies to some extent. When you can blend your own inner polarities, you manifest harmonious and wholesome union with your twin.

Embracing and acceptance is the key. Be in conscious awareness and understand that the answers are always within. In spiritual reality, As within, so Without.

I AM CLOSE & NEAR TO YOU

My love! When you chose this page, it means that you and I are moving closer to each other!

It can also be a sign that you are becoming more positively connected to me, that your timelines are merging for an upcoming reunion, that old resentments have been healed, that I am thinking about you, dreaming about you, or much likely, that you are attracting a face-to-face meeting!

For positive results stay in optimistic expectation and allow the subtle feeling of euphoria and happiness to take you ahead.

INNER CHILD HEALING

Dear, the inner child trauma holds the answers to what you are going through currently. Any incident that happened in the past with you or me requires healing.

Did you know that your relationship with your caretakers as a child crucially influences your current adult relations and partnerships? This is how everyone "learn" how to be and respond in relationships and what to expect from their spouse when they've grown up.

Many adults have "inner child trauma". The inner child in its original state stays with innocence, creativity, and playfulness.

So how have you been feeling recently? The inner child can often be afraid of burdened responsibility, afraid that someone will take their love away if they do something silly, like others are angry with them or like no one is giving attention to their needs for safety, care, and well-being.

When the inner child is sad, you will notice subconscious self-sabotage, irrational actions and intense emotions coming at surface.

Observe and listen to your inner child. There might be repressed issue. Another sign from this page is, my inner child could be the one in agony.

In nutshell, this situation revolves around the inner child trauma issue - the innocent side of you and mine. There are unhealed traumas. Visit your inner child and mine and check out what are their needs are at this very moment.

MAGNETIC ATTRACTION

Darling, there's a strong magnetic pull between us.

You've received this page because you feel an intense pull towards me. In simple words, you share chemistry with me. This creates profound pleasurable feelings that allure us to each other.

In contrast, this page could be a sign that the lack of chemistry is causing our relationship conflicts and personal resentments. If there was chemistry initially, it may be restored by putting efforts to our connection. Passion evokes, and romance can be brought back by playfulness, quality time together, regular communication, and affectionate gestures.

Ask the universe to guide you as you make crucial decisions about rekindling this chemistry.

CALL YOUR TWIN FLAME

Your prayers, affirmations, and visualization helps us be in harmonious union.

This page guides you to wholeheartedly call me into your life. You can do this by prayer, affirmations, and creative visualizations.
It also means working on yourself so that you enhance the qualities you're seeking in me. For example, if you want me to have a great sense of humor or empathy, develop this within yourself, first.
Remember, like attracts like, which is of calling in your Twin Flame in the union.

UNLEASH YOURSELF

Love, it's time to take back control of your life!
It seems that you've given too much control to someone else, or maybe you feel suffocated in your career or particular relationship. As you bring your focus inside yourself, you'll feel the particular areas where this message applies to you. You can even ask yourself, "In what ways do I feel restrained?"
Trust the answers you receive.

This page comes to you from me as a message that the universe has heard your prayers for a profound love and our harmonious union.
To attract passionate love, though, you must first allow yourself to embrace deep feelings. In doing so, you may come across areas of your life where you carry resentments. Simply by acknowledging these areas, you bring peace to the incident and allow for the universe to help you.

As you dedicate yourself to take back the control of your life, your emotions will naturally cordial and renewed. This leads to a profound ability to love yourself, me, and your upcoming experiences.

ARE YOU REALLY COMMITED TO LOVE

Dear, the universe is asking to observe how committed you are to love and our Twin Flame journey.

True love means commitment without any conditions. We give ourselves wholeheartedly in the hope that love will endure and last forever. Love is an act of faith. Align and resonate yourself with love and know that your life will be happy for it.

BREAK IS ESSENTIAL

Dear, we all have universal need to take rest. Don't beat up yourself with too much expectation and burnout. Everything will be alright.

We are at our best when we balance out all areas of our lives. Love yourself and the people in your life enough to create an environment that allows all of them the opportunity to take care of their needs. When you are relaxed and refreshed, you are at our best and able to fully acknowledge all that the life has to offer.

DREAM MORE OFTEN

Sweetheart, when we start dreaming, everything is possible.
Make sure you no longer catch hold of things that have passed and no longer exist. Everybody has a past that has helped to evolve who they are right now. The history cannot be erased. Accept the past and look forward to the future. Set intentions and dream massive. By doing this, you will eradicate the purging of repressed negativity from the past, creating blockage in our union. Having intentions help us to focus on what is crucial.

EMBRACE THE PRESENT

Love, you attract love by enjoying the moment fully.
Every situation has an opportunity to evolve and manifest love.
Sometimes there are incidents that seem like obstacles and don't make any sense at the time. It is important that you embrace and fully acknowledge what is happening currently so that you can learn the soul lessons that you are being taught currently. Ask the universe to give you signs of what is crucial in present and clear the energetic blockage between you and me.

TWIN FLAME MERGE

You and I are always in energetic soul connection on the non-physical realm.

As we are one soul in two bodies, we emit and are on the "same vibration" and hence always influencing each other and our higher selves are "quietly communicating" with each other. You might be picking up on my experiences currently: my emotions and fears, my uncertainties.

Yet another sign for this page is that you and I are entering into or evolving in the Union Stage of our journey. This being said, our energies, chakras and timelines are being merged with each other ever more, including connecting our higher chakras.

Union is an energetic phenomenon without boundaries, time frames and conditions, because it depends on your approach and your soul's framework. The union stage is all about bringing us closer, back to wholeness as two humans. Hence, it involves clearing apprehension- based emotions and allowing you to choose frequency of love to unite.

Note down that when you choose love always, you are choosing Union. When you choose apprehension, you are repelling further away. Just know that the fear causes separation. So, every second ask, is this taking me closer to love? Or repelling away from it? Your intuition is the only compass you require.

Another sign when you receive this page is that you are thinking if your shadow work, intentions, and affirmations are affecting me or not. The answer is definitely yes! Although you may not see it on a 3D physical level yet, but you definitely are.

ENERGETIC CORDS

Honey, there has been trails and tribulations for you because there are still energetic cords connected to old relations with your soul or mine's.

Whenever anyone engages in closeness, whether it is sexual or emotionally profound. Energetic cords of attachments are form between the two people. These cords are like having a telephone line into the other person's existence and them to you. It keeps you energetically interconnected.

For the Twin Flame voyage to love and union, this is troublesome because our souls are operating to purify us in the light of unconditional love - which is the state at which complete reunion occurs.

Currently, your soul is functioning to reflect that attachments to exes or other karmic acquaintances need to be cut and cleansed in order to make path for what you have been desiring for.

It might also associate with soul contracts. Many people are connected to these through marriage, engagements, promises to one another.

This operate similar to attachments. The issue with this aspect is that this is not something you can simply plan or think your way out of. It compels you to terminate the contracts and cut energetic cords vibrationally. This will commence you to a new happy chapter.

Another sign for this page that I may be the one who's dealing with karmic cords, association, and connections.

There might also be apprehension-based connection between us that are being purged for clearing out. This must be released to elevate your vibration too - to open to a elevated state of bond.

An easy yet profound way to cut energetic cords and connection, is to get a piece of string and cut it with an aim that you are clearing the connection.

YES, SOON

When you draw this page, you may have been emiting mixed signals out to the universe. Maybe you have been praying for something, then in apprehension then abandoning out your desire. Maybe you have had second thoughts about whether your desire can really manifest.

Make a solid choice, or if you're not sure, pray for clarification in the form of signs or synchronicity that will help you know what is truly to your highest good both currently and in the future.

The issue is that if you don't make a choice, if you get dwell in second thoughts or don't accept to yourself what you are truly desiring, the universe cannot send you what you want. It's like trying to click "play" and "pause" at the same time - the mix signals cancel each other out.

Ask yourself, why are you afraid of choosing? Why are you having second thoughts? Then work to let go the apprehension energy so you can have clarity. Always to listen to your heart. Observe in your heart what you truly yearn for?

Nothing is out of your hand - know what your heart desires, and pray to universe to help you to manifest it. Don't belittle your desires because you have been asked to be rational.

Currently it is the time to make your solid choice. In this present time, send out to the universe what you truly want. Release your doubts, and set your goals firmly. This assists to make way for it to show up - the universe will always answer to you, so make sure you are confident on what you want.

ASCENSION STAGE

Sugar, your soul wants you to evolve from current situation. Something that is happening in your life is connected to a *soul lesson* you are being signaled to master.

Try to see yourself from a 3rd person's perspective. Try to observe what might be the higher reason of what is happening? What lesson might your soul be desiring for you to put efforts on?

Are you being motivated to learn self-love & appreciation or making healthy boundaries – because others might be mistreating you or taking you for granted? Are you being challenged to move forward to learn as a co-creator of life - through circumstances being distressing?

Are you being challenged to master that you are never really alone at soul level- by going through physical separation? Look for the soul lessons in your circumstances and you can start to level into a harmonious path. Because you and your soul will be operating in order to evolve and ascension together.

And if you feel stuck, ask your soul if there is a simple way for you to comprehend what you need. Remember that no matter how tough it may seem, your soul will never put you into anything you are not proficient of tackling.

But it may impel you to surpass your comfort zone, impel you to shatter your own boundaries, to evolve and ascension on your abilities and reach into an elevated state of living for future.

Currently it can feel hard when your soul is impelling you to go further, but understand that this is ultimately for your own good.

Remember, that anyone else connected in your soul lesson is as a soul doing it to evolve you. Often, someone who challenge you the most are the people who have signed up to evolve and assist you in learning important soul lessons in life.

SUMMON ME

Currently it would help you bring me closer by fixing your desire and yearning to invite me into your life. By summoning me it will also send your firm intentions to the universe to bring us in union.

For a wonderful outcome write down a note with pen/pencil and paper. Select the words that feel heartfelt to you. An example would be: *"I now summon my divine Twin Flame into my life on all levels, in the here and present. And so, it is"*.

Put this message under your pillow and understand that it will be manifesting like a miracle, calling in me like a magnet.

Due to the *free will*, my higher self may have been anticipating for permission or confirmation to fully step forward into your life.

Maybe because you've sent me mixed intentions with resentments or fear and I want to make sure you really are willing and wanting for me to show up, or maybe because you haven't expected yet.

In nutshell, writing out this message is a definite way to summon me in.

LOOK OUT FOR THE SIGNS SENT TO YOU REPEATEDLY

Sweetheart, look out for the signs you are been sent! In case you are seeing coins or feathers, seeing repeating angelic number sequences such as 11:11, 222, 555, noticing helpful love quotes or other signs along your way. The universe is communicating to you.

So, ask yourself - what repetitive synchronicities have you been noticing lately? What repetitive quotes have you read or heard? What signs and messages are approaching?

You are always being communicated- love, help and nudge and universe is always functioning to get your attention. The more you pay focus to the signs and synchronicities on your journey, the more you will receive messages like this.

Universe, guardian angels, and my higher self arc always with you and functioning to show you the unconditional love we feel for you. If you have doubts on what something is trying to tell you, ask for clarity or for the sign to be given in a different way.

In a nutshell, these signs seek to tell you that you are not alone. That you are loved and desired. That there really is a reason to your experiences, and that there is truly great things waiting for you.

MEETING IN DREAMS

Dear, you may have noticed this before, but currently you have been having experiences during dreams and REM sleep that are not just usual dreams. There are signs functioning to reach you.

You might already realize that you are not just a physical body. You are a soul, a being of energy having a 3D life. When you sleep, you can travel across in your *astral body* in different dimensional realms - on a different level of consciousness.

You might have experienced this kind of spiritual experience while you're awake too - because when you and I interconnect remotely, our astral self is engaged.

Whether it occurs in a dream, meditation or when you're awake. This is how you are capable to feel me, without being physically in union – it is our non-physical self communication.

Start to observe what experiences you have been having during your sleep - there is much to know from this. Universe and I are always trying to give you signs through dreams and astral travel. Pay focus to repetitive image, signs, and messages.

Understand that you can start to embrace your abilities more straightforwardly, too. You can practice lucid dreaming techniques to fully gain from your night sleep incidents.

When you have learned astral travel, you can stay in connection with me as if you were always tangibly here in union.

YOU ARE DOING GREAT

My love, I am so happy for you! You are doing such wonderful job and have made profound improvement. Pamper yourself with rewards, the way I wish to celebrate you!

Make sure you appreciate your triumphs over small and big goals, and cherish yourself for being real. I am so proud of who you *are* completely. Not just what actions you take. Even your being, too.

With this page, I wish to give you my love and acknowledgment. You deserve self-pampering.

Remember that universe will be sending you a sign or message of triumph in some way very soon in the physical.

Another sign for this page is to know that other people can be absorbed with their own conflicts and anxieties and don't know how to bring out their acknowledgement.

Currently, there is a person in your life who is happy for you and acknowledge you, even if they don't know how to express it freely.

ESSENCE OF UNION

My dear, an awakened relationship isn't just about a soulful connection, it's when couples can spend countless time being amazed at colors of sunset, stars gazing, random outburst of laughter, relaxing at their favorite cafeteria or restaurant and spontaneous love making.

It is profoundly about being able to trust each other, to be able & willing to carry safe loving space, while being fully vulnerable to communicate completely about the most distressing, disturbing, and debatable topics that come up to the surface.

If one comes short of the empathy, respect and kindness, the intimate dance is just a sleeping dance and not an awakened dance. At the awakened level, everything is mirrored and the more a person can address & function on the repressed agony & deep wounds, the more they are allowing light & love to heal each other. To become complete and whole in love & light is union.

PATIENCE, MY LOVE

Love, divine timing is at work in our love life. Our Twin flame relationship requires patience, as there are numerous attributes involved.
My *freewill* choices are beyond your or the universe's control, as is the receptive alignment of us both for harmonious physical union. This page comes to you as a reminder that our relationship and union are *worth waiting for*.

Divine timing is a universal law that is always in function. If we try our human will and force or try to control things to happen, we become out of alignment with the manifestation and create blockages between us and our union.
Likewise, if we fear, "When will I meet my Twin Flame?" we put *doubt* and *lack* energy out into universe.

The universe has heard and answered your prayers for our union, and is working behind the scenes to get this to you. Your duty is to hear and follow your intuition, even if it seems trivial to your desire.

Your insights are like a guiding compass, leading you to the path of answered prayers. Follow your intuition and have faith in the timing of our union.

EPILOGUE

To begin with, it is a sheer delight, at that point, it is comforting, at that point challenging, at that point destroying some time recently it returns to be challenging, at that point comforting and back to sheer delight. The Twin Flame Path is the foremost wondrous thing that can happen for us on our otherworldly way. We meet this individual that tears our heart wide open and turns our entirety world, as we knew it, upside down. Everything falls separated. We are shaken up profoundly in our convictions and feelings surface in a concentrated, we seem not to accept would be conceivable. The life we thought we were very upbeat with all of a sudden does not make any sense any longer. All we need is to be with that other individual, no matter what. The Twin Flame Relationship was considered very rare, and not a well-known subject, indeed within the spiritual world.